Aman Chiu 著

# 圖像
# 速學英語冠詞

Learn articles in English
*through pictures*

商務印書館

圖像速學英語冠詞

Learn articles in English through pictures

作　　者：Aman Chiu

責任編輯：黃家麗

出　　版：商務印書館 (香港) 有限公司

香港筲箕灣耀興道 3 號東滙廣場 8 樓

http://www.commercialpress.com.hk

發　　行：香港聯合書刊物流有限公司

香港新界大埔汀麗路 36 號中華商務印刷大廈 3 字樓

印　　刷：美雅印刷製本有限公司

九龍官塘榮業街 6 號海濱工業大廈 4 樓 A 室

版　　次：2015 年 5 月第 1 版第 1 次印刷

© 2015 商務印書館 (香港) 有限公司

ISBN 978 962 07 1950 9

Printed in Hong Kong

# 目錄
## CONTENTS

# Section 1: The Basics of Articles

 冠詞基本知識

# 何謂冠詞？

冠詞是虛詞，本身不能單獨使用，只能用在名詞前面，在句子裏對名詞起限定作用，幫助指明名詞的含義。

# 冠詞種類

冠詞有三種，一種是 indefinite article（不定冠詞），另一種是 definite article（定冠詞），還有一種是易被忽略的 zero article（零冠詞）。不定冠詞有兩個形式，即是 a 和 an；定冠詞 the 只有一個形式；而零冠詞指名詞前面沒有 a、an（不定冠詞）及 the（定冠詞），也沒有其他限定詞，它也是冠詞的一種，在語言學上多以符號 ø 表示。

# 冠詞誤用

冠詞用法看似簡單，卻是中國人常犯的英語錯誤，其誤用現象可分三類：該用沒用、畫蛇添足和混淆不清。

(1) **該用沒用**，即是該用冠詞但沒用，這在各種冠詞誤用所佔比例最大。比如說 "變成一個壞習慣"，我們完全可省去數量詞 "一個" 而不影響表達，但 to become a bad habit 卻不能省去 a。中國人用英語名詞會受中文影響，有時又記不清固定片語，很易漏掉該用的冠詞。

(2) **畫蛇添足**，不該用冠詞時用多了。中國人易在固定片語中多用了冠詞，原因是不完全掌握片語、記憶偏差或受母語干擾，比如會將 for instance 說成 for an instance，原因是從 "舉個例子說" 的中文思維直譯英文。

(3) **混淆不清**，即是在行文造句中混淆定冠詞 the 和不定冠詞 a / an，或混淆 a 和 an。混淆現象可以這樣解釋：學習者不知道以子音音素開頭的單數可數名詞之前該用 a，以母音音素開頭的單數可數名詞之前該用 an，或只知道以母音開頭的單數名詞之前可用 an，而不知道這裏的 "母音" 是指母音音素。混淆 a / an 和 the 大多是由於學習者不清楚哪個單數名詞的所指是泛指還是特指。

學好冠詞是提升英語能力的關鍵所在。本書精要地闡釋英語冠詞的用法，並針對以上三點中國人常犯的毛病作出扼要說明，將定冠詞、不定冠詞、零冠詞的各種用途清楚明瞭地整理出來，幫助讀者將已懂的知識有條理地重溫一遍，並對不曾學過或未能清晰了解的部份作出深入了解。書中通過圖像和大量簡明實用的例子，讓讀者一看就明，一明就能自行模仿應用。當中一些容易混淆或使用錯誤的冠詞更會附加注解，說明其於文法上的正確用法和注意事項，以幫助讀者有效掌握冠詞，從而提升英語的整體能力。

# 01 PRONUNCIATION 冠詞的發音

## ⚡ 1.1 a 和 an 的發音

用 a 或 an 取決於後面的詞的讀音，不看它開頭的字母。

**1.1.1 a 用於以 consonant（子音）來起音的單詞之前，一般讀作 /e/。**

 例
- a boy
- a cat
- a European
- a hat
- a hero
- a history class
- a uniform
- a university

※ 注意，區別 a 及 an 的用法時，要特別注意的是發音。一個單字，即使字首是子音字母，但實際發母音時，仍要用 an。例：an hour /en əʊə/。（詳見下節）

相反地，一個單字，字首若是母音字母，但實際發子音時需要用 a。例如以 u 字母開始，起音像 you 的單詞之前用 a：a European、a uniform、a university 等。類似例子還有：

**形容詞：**

| ubiquitous | unanimous | uniformed | unifying | unilateral | unique |
|------------|-----------|-----------|----------|------------|--------|
| united | universal | urinal | urinary | usable | used |
| useful | useless | usual | usually | utilitarian | utopian |

名詞：

| unicorn | uniform | uniformity | unilateralist | union | unisex |
| --- | --- | --- | --- | --- | --- |
| unit | universe | university | uranium | urine | usage |
| use | user | usurper | utensil | uterus | utility |

## 1.1.2　an 用於以 vowel（母音）來起音的單詞之前，一般讀作 /en/。

- an egg
- an English teacher
- an elephant
- an empty box
- an honest man
- an hour
- an island
- an octopus
- an old man
- an onion
- an umbrella

※ 注意，以 h 開始，但 h 不發音的單詞之前要用 an。例如以上 an
hour、 an honest man 兩例。類似例子還有：

形容詞：honourable 、 honorary 、 hourly

名詞：honour 、 heir

## 1.1.3　以母音來起音的縮寫詞之前要用 an。

- an IQ test
- an SOS call
- an MBA degree
- an NBA player

※ 注意，字首若是母音字母，但實際發子音時需要用 a，
例如：a UFO 、 a US senator。

# 1.2 the 的發音

**不論指人或物，單數或複數，後接名詞以子音或母音起音也好，定冠詞 the 的形式都不變。**

### 1.2.1 以子音來起音的單詞之前讀 /ðə/。

- the cat
- the man
- the British Council
- the government

### 1.2.2 以母音來起音的單詞之前（即一般前面用 an 的詞）讀 /ði/。

- the end
- the eye
- the house
- the idol
- the island
- the umbrella

### 1.2.3 在特別強調時讀 /ðiː/，例如用於想對方特別注意 the 之後的名詞。

- Do you mean the / ðiː / Faye Wang, the singer?
  你指的是歌手王菲嗎？
- If you have any further questions about this, Johnson is the / ðiː / person to ask.
  你若對這方面還有其他問題，即管找莊遜。

#  1.3 用法速查表
## Speed check

**冠詞發音：**

| 場合 | 例子 |
| --- | --- |
| a 用在以子音來起音的單詞前，一般讀作 /e/ | a boy<br>a cat<br>a European<br>a university |
| an 用在以母音來起音的單詞前，一般讀作 /en/。 | an egg<br>an elephant<br>an hour<br>an umbrella |
| the 用在以子音來起音的單詞前，讀 /ðə/。 | the cat<br>the man<br>the British Council<br>the government |
| the 用在以母音來起音的單詞前（即一般前面用 an 的詞），讀 /ði/。 | the end<br>the eye<br>the honour<br>the island |

# 02 INDEFINITE ARTICLES *A / AN* : BASIC USAGE 不定冠詞 A / AN 的基本用法

**a 和 an 只用於單數可數名詞之前，兩者在意義上沒有區別。**

## ⚡ 2.1 怎樣用
### Usage

**用途**

**A** **表示 "一個"。**

a 和 an 只用於單數可數名詞之前，兩者在意義上沒有區別。

**例**
- a book and a pencil  一本書和一支鉛筆
- an egg / an elephant  一隻雞蛋 / 一頭大象
- I'd like an apple. 我想要一個蘋果。

⊕ **比較中英文：**

a / an 意思相當於中文的「一個、一張、一支、一隻、一本、一輛……」等等，例如：

| | | |
|---|---|---|
| a bed（一張牀） | a bridge（一座橋） | a building（一棟大樓） |
| a car（一輛汽車） | a horse（一匹馬） | a panda（一隻熊貓） |

**用途**

## 表示一般而不是特定的人或物。

a / an 有不確定的意義，即是所說的人或事物對聽者或讀者來說可能是不知道、不認識的，它包含了「任何一個」或「是哪一個也無關重要」的意思。

- I met an old friend on my way back home. 我在回家的路上遇上一位舊朋友。（但不必說是哪一位朋友。）
- I had a nightmare last night. 我昨晚做了一場噩夢。（但不必說是怎樣的噩夢。）
- We went to see an exhibition last Sunday. 我們上星期日去參觀了一個展覽。（但不必說是哪類型的展覽。）

⊕ **比較中英文：**

在英語裏，單數可數名詞前一般都需要加上不定冠詞，例如 ride a horse / drive a car。中文裏沒有冠詞的概念，"騎馬" 或 "開車" 一般不會畫蛇添足地說成 "騎一匹馬"，"開一輛車"。反過來說，英語的冠詞卻不能隨意刪掉，例如 "他是學生。" 這句話必須說成 He is a student. ，而不能說 He is student. 。

**用途 C**

## 代表一類人或事物。

a / an 也表示「該類中的一個例子」,用來泛指某類人或物,但不具體說明何人何物。

- He became a school teacher. 他當上了教師。
- Mr Smith is an engineer. 史密夫先生是工程師。
- She is a Buddhist. 她是佛教徒。

用 a / an 作一般陳述時,常採用如詞典為詞條下定義的形式。

- A teacher is a person who teaches at a school. 老師在學校教書。
- A knife is a tool used for cutting. 刀是用來切東西的工具。

※ 注意,當我們要表示的是「該類中的一個例子」,許多不可數名詞也可以與 a / an 連用。

- This is a very good tea. Is it Long Jing?
  這種茶非常好,是龍井嗎?

**用途 D**

## 對人或事物進行分類。

a / an 可以隨意與名人作品、特別名稱或品牌等連用,以對人或事物進行分類,當中也包含「該類中的一例」的意思。

- a Mo Yan novel 莫言的一部小說
- a Shakespeare play 一齣莎士比亞戲劇
- a Chang Dai-chien painting 一幅張大千的畫
- He's an Aisin Gioro. 他是個姓愛新覺羅的人。
- It's an Ang Li film. 這是李安的一部電影。
- She was wearing a D&G gown. 她穿上了一襲 D&G 晚裝。
- Leonardo Da Vinci was a Renaissance artist.
  達文西是文藝復興時期的藝術家。

用途

## 表示某某人。

a / an 可用在稱呼（如 Miss 、 Mr 、 Mrs 、 Dr 等）前面，指說話者不認識的某某人，含有 a certain（某某）的意思。

- A Mr Robinson is waiting for you.
  一位姓羅賓遜的先生在等你。
- A Mrs Wang called you this morning.
  一位姓王的太太早上給你打電話。

☞ 比較 7.1 A 姓名

用途

## 表示病痛。

a / an 可與某些疾病傷痛名稱連用。

- a cold / a stuffy nose / a running nose / a sore throat
  感冒 / 鼻塞 / 流鼻水 / 喉嚨痛
- a headache / an earache / a backache / a stomachache
  頭痛 / 耳痛 / 背痛 / 胃痛
- a fractured arm / a broken leg 斷了的手臂 / 斷了的腿
- I've got a sore throat. 我喉嚨痛。
- Swiss researchers have discovered that the brain adjusts
  quickly to a broken limb.
  瑞士的研究員發現人一旦遭遇斷肢腦袋會迅速作出適應。

※ 注意，有些時候不定冠詞可以乾脆不用。

- Don't catch (a) cold. 別受涼。

• I've had (a) stomachache the whole morning.
我整個早上都在胃痛。

※ 注意，以複數形式出現的疾病名稱，如 measles（痲疹）、mumps（流行性腮腺炎）則屬例外。

☞ 比較 10.1 G 疾病

 用途

# 表示頻度。

a / an 與表示量度的詞語連用，表示 "每" 的意思。

 • three meals a day 一日三餐
• We have six classes a day. 我們一天上六節課。
• He drives the car at sixty-five miles an hour.
他以每小時 65 公里的速度駕駛。

※ 注意，如果特別強調 "每一"，則需要用 per 代替 a / an。
• He takes seven meals per day. 他每天要吃七餐。

 用途

# 自然成對的名詞。

有些名詞本身是成雙成對，可視之為一體。a / an 僅置於這類成對名詞的第一個名詞前，不用置於第二個名詞前。

- a knife and fork 一副刀叉：
  Would you eat a hotdog with a knife and fork?
  你會用（一副）刀叉來吃熱狗嗎？
- a hat and coat 一套衣帽：
  A man in a hat and coat gestured me over.
  一個穿戴同樣衣帽的男人朝我打手勢叫我過去。
- a cup and saucer 一套杯碟：
  Put a tea cup and saucer to the right of the drinking glass.
  把一套茶杯碟放在玻璃杯的右邊。

※ 注意，此類名詞之後若接動詞，必須作單數的變化。

- I bought a beautiful knife and fork, which was very expensive.
  我買了一副漂亮的刀叉，它們非常貴。

※ 注意，a knife and fork 表示的是一個整體。另一個說法是 a knife and a fork（一把刀和一把叉），所表示的是兩樣不同的東西，若後接動詞便要用複數變化。

※ 注意，如果兩個名詞並非自然成對，每個名詞前都必須要加上不定冠詞 a / an，並且當作兩個獨立個體，當成複數。

- I bought a cup and a fork, which were very expensive.
  我買了一隻杯和一把叉子，它們非常貴。

☞ 比較 12.1 F 成對詞語

## 2.2 用法速查表
### Speed check

**不定冠詞的基本用法：**

| 場合 | 例子 |
| --- | --- |
| A 表示一個 | a pen / an apple |
| B 表示一般而不是特定的人或物 | I met an old friend on my way back home. |
| C 代表一類人或事物 | His father is a teacher. |
| D 對人或事物進行分類 | It's an Ang Li film. |
| E 表示某某人 | A Mr Robinson is waiting for you. |
| F 表示疾病 | I've got a sore throat. |
| G 表示頻率程度 | We have six classes a day. |
| H 自然成對的名詞 | I bought a beautiful knife and fork. |

# 03 INDEFINITE ARTICLES *A / AN* :
## SPECIAL USAGE 不定冠詞 A / AN 的特殊用法

 ## 3.1 怎樣用
### Usage

用途

## A 與 what 連用表示感歎。

a / an 與可數名詞連用，位於 what 之後以表達感歎的語氣。

例
- What a liar you are! 你可是個騙子！
- What a surprise! 好驚喜啊！

可數名詞前一般加上修飾語以增強語氣。

例
- What a lovely kitten! 多可愛的小貓！
- What a fabulous film! 極好的電影！

Quite a ... 亦可用來表示感歎。

例
- Quite a tiring trip it is! 好累的旅程！
- Quite a difficult situation it is! 好困難的處境！

用途

## 與 such 連用表示強調。

在 such 後面用 a / an 除了有感歎成份之外，還能強調程度。

例
- You are such a liar! 你真是個大話精！
- It was such a great dinner! 那是多棒的一頓飯！
- His girlfriend is such a big mouth! 他女友可真多嘴！
- You're such a strong little boy and I'm proud of you.
  你真是個勇敢的小男孩，我以你為傲。

用途

## 特別修辭手法。

用途 a / an 與數量詞 many 連用，後接單數名詞，同樣能起強調作用。

- Many a young man has fallen in love with her.
  她可不乏裙下之臣。
- Many a flower is born to blush unseen.
  許多花朵生來就開着沒人欣賞。

※ 注意，這是一種特別修辭手法，包含強烈的文學氣息。有人會認為這種用法過時，一般場合採用不多。

※ 注意，這類名詞之後若接動詞，必須作單數的變化。因此以上兩例中的 has 和 is 不可說成 have 和 are。

用途

## 用在固定片語中。

某些固定片語中必須使用不定冠詞。

（與數量有關）

- a little 一點 / a few 一些 / a lot of 很多 / a pile of 一堆 / a great many 許多

（與時間有關）

- in a hurry 匆忙地 / in a minute 一會 / Just a moment 請稍等片刻 / in a moment 馬上 / quite a while 相當長的一段時間 / in a short while 一會 / all of a sudden 忽然

（與分類有關）

- a type of / a kind of / a sort of 一類（一種）

（have + 名詞）

- have a go 試試看 / have a rest 歇一歇 / have a look 看一下 / have a ride 坐一下車 / have a talk 談一下 / have a swim 去游泳 / have a wash 洗一洗

（其他）

- as a rule 一般 / as a result of 由於 / as a matter of fact 事實上 / in a word 一句話（簡單地說）/ worth a try 值得一試 / do me a favour 請幫個忙 / keep an eye on 密切注意

#  3.2 用法速查表
## Speed check

**不定冠詞的特殊用法：**

| 場合 | 例子 |
|------|------|
| **A** 表示感歎 | What a liar you are!<br>How a brave boy he is! |
| **B** 表示強調 | You are such a liar! |
| **C** 特別修辭手法 | There is many a student.<br>= There are many students. |
| **D** 用在固定片語中 | a little / a few / a lot of / all of a sudden |

# 04 DEFINITE ARTICLE *THE* :
## BASIC USAGE 定冠詞 THE 的基本用法

定冠詞 the 具有確定意思，用來特指人或事物，表示名詞所指的人
或事物是同類中特定的一個，以別於同類中其他人或事物。它可以
和單數、複數名詞，也可以和不可數名詞連用。

 ## 4.1 怎樣用
### Usage

用途

 **A** **談話雙方都知道的人或事物。**

the 用於說話雙方具有共識的特定名詞之前。

 例
- Where is the teacher? 老師在哪裏？
- Open the windows, please. 請打開窗。
- What's the weather like out there? 外面的天氣怎樣？
- The pens I gave you were bought in Paris.
  我給你的鋼筆是在巴黎買的。
- The chair I was sitting on was shaky. 我坐的那張椅子不穩。

⊕ **比較中英文**

定冠詞基本相當於中文的"這個"、"那個"。它具有指向性和排他性。形象地說，它就是一個箭頭，如果沒有它，就不知道說哪個事物。

**用途**

## 複述上文提過的人或事物。

第一次提到時用不定冠詞 a / an，第二次提到時用定冠詞 the。

- She bought a book. The book is about UFOs.
  她買了一本書，那是一本關於不明飛行物體的書。
- "Can I have a glass of water, please?" Colin asked.
- "I put the glass of water on the table already," the maid replied.

  "可以請你給我一杯水嗎？"科林說。

  "我已經把一杯水在放桌上了。"傭人答道。

※ 注意，如冠詞與名詞之間出現修飾語，句中仍會沿用不定冠詞。

- "I'd like a really big glass of water, please," Colin said.
  我想要一大杯水，可以嗎？"科林說。
- "I put a really big glass of water on the table already,"
  the maid replied.
  "我已把一大杯水放在桌上了。"傭人答道。

**用途**

## 獨一無二的事物。

the 用於世上獨一無二的事物。

- the sun / the moon / the earth / the sky  太陽 / 月亮 / 地球 / 天空
- the atmosphere / the universe / the solar system / the galaxy
  大氣層 / 宇宙 / 太陽系 / 銀河系
- The sun rises in the east. 太陽從東方升起。
- The earth goes round the sun. 地球圍繞太陽作公轉。

※ 注意，earth 一般不大寫，除非它與其他星體名稱一起使用，如 Jupiter is farther from the sun than Earth is.（木星比地球離太陽遠。）。這裏的 Earth 作為專有名稱，不需要加冠詞。然而，如果 earth 的前面有定冠詞 the，那麼它一定要小寫，如 The moon came between the earth and the sun.（月球在地球與太陽之間。）。

## 樂器。

the 用在表示樂器的名詞之前。

- She plays the piano very well. 她鋼琴彈得非常好。
- Helen teaches the flute. 海倫是教長笛的。
- Colin is learning the saxophone. 科林正在學吹薩克管。
- I practice the clarinet an hour a day.
  我每天練一個小時的單簧管。
- Stop beating the drum! 別再打鼓了！
- The oboe plays the main theme. 主題旋律由雙簧管演奏。
- My father took up the violin in his retirement.
  我爸爸退休後開始學拉小提琴。

※ 注意，如樂器名詞表示具體的器物或表示課程時，則不加 the。

- They bought a piano last week. 他們上星期買了一台鋼琴。
- Helen teaches piano in school. 海倫在學校裏教鋼琴。

※ 注意，某些以漢語拼音標示的中國樂名稱前面，可不加冠詞，例如 to play erhu / sanxian（彈二胡 / 三弦）。

**用途**

# E 方向與方位。

the 用在表示方向或方位的名詞前。

- on the left / right 在左 / 右邊
- in the east / in the west 在東方（面）/ 在西方（面）
- The wind is coming from the west. 風從西面來。
- Towards the north the woods turn into pine trees.
  向北樹林就成了松樹林。
- They hid themselves at the back of the door. 他們躲藏在門後。

※ 注意，如直接用於動詞後則不用加上 the。

- The windows face south. 窗戶朝南。
- Which way is west? 哪邊是西？

※ 注意，方位詞成對使用構成平行結構時不用加上 the。

- They drove through the desert from west to east.
  他們自西向東開車穿越這片沙漠。

**用途**

# F 身體部位或人體結構。

the 用於 "表示身體部位或人體結構的名詞前"。

- She caught me by the arm. 她抓住了我的手臂。
- He received a blow on the head. 他頭部捱了一擊。
- Her father took her by the hand. 她爸爸牽着她的手。
- This paper investigates the congenital deformities of the uterus.
  此文針對子宮先天性畸形現象進行調查。

※ 注意，以上定冠詞不能由 possessive pronoun（所有格代詞）取代：

✗ She caught me by my arm.
✗ He received a blow on his head.
✗ Her father took her by her hand.

※ 注意，在一連串名詞中，只需在第一個名詞前加 the 即可，不需要逐一重複用冠詞。

- This paper investigates the congenital deformities of the uterus, ovaries, and fallopian tubes.
  此文針對子宮、卵巢、 輸卵管的先天性畸形現象進行調查。

## ⚡ 4.2 用法速查表
### Speed check

### 定冠詞的基本用法：

| 場合 | 例子 |
|------|------|
| A 談話雙方都知道的人或事物 | Where's the remote control? 遙控器在哪裏？ |
| B 複述上文提過的人或事物 | He bought a book. The book is about aliens. 他買了一本書。那是一本關於外星人的書。 |
| C 獨一無二的事物 | the sky / the moon 天空／月球 |
| D 樂器 | to play the piano 彈鋼琴 |
| E 方向或方位 | the Far East 遠東 |
| F 身體部份或人體結構 | He took me by the hand. 他牽着我的手。 |

# 05 DEFINITE ARTICLE *THE* AND REFERRING TO A GROUP
## 定冠詞 THE 與特指群體

the 可與不同語法項目組合起來，表示 "一類事物或特指群體"。

## 5.1 怎樣用
### Usage

用途

**A** **the + 單數可數名詞：強調整個類別。**

the 用在單數可數名詞前，表示 "一類人或事物"，強調整個類別。

例
- The crocodile is very dangerous. 鱷魚是極度危險的。
- The bottlenose dolphin is one of the most well-known dolphin species around the world.
  寬吻海豚是世上最著名的海豚物種之一。

※ 注意，不定冠詞 + 單數名詞，不帶冠詞的複數名詞也可表示一類人或物。

☞ 另見 2 C 代表一類人或事物
☞ 另見 9 A 泛指一類人

# B the + 複數可數名詞：特指的群體。

很多複數可數名詞，在特指從社會中區分出來的某部份人時，可加 the 表示。

- the workers 工人們 / the unions 工會 / the bosses 老闆們
- Karl Kautsky: *The Intellectuals and the Workers* (1903)
  《知識份子和工人階級》卡爾・考茨基著

同樣，與複數名詞連用，指整個群體。

- They are the teachers of this school. 他們是本校的教師。
  （指全體教師）

⊕ **比較：**
- They are teachers of this school. 他們是本校的教師。
  （指部份教師）

# C the + 形容詞：特指的群體。

與某些形容詞連用，表示一類人。

- the blind 盲人 / the deaf 聾人 / the dumb 啞巴
- the wounded 傷者 / the sick 患者 / the disabled 殘障人士 /
  the handicapped 傷殘人士 / the challenged 身心障礙者
- the young 年輕人 / the aged 老人 / the elderly 長者
- the living 活着的人 / the dead 死者 / the living dead 活死人
- the rich 富人 / the poor 窮人 / the underprivileged 被剝奪了基
  本權利的人或無權無勢的人 / the disadvantaged 貧困的人
- The Hong Kong Society For the Deaf 香港聾人福利促進會

也可用來表示某種抽象概念。

- the good 美好的事 / the impossible 不可能發生的事 /
  the unknown 未知的東西 / the unheard of 前所未聞的事 /
  the unexpected 出乎意料的事 / the supernatural 超自然現象

用途

# D the + 集合名詞：特指的群體。

與集合名詞連用，來對特指的群體作一般陳述。

- the police 警員；警方 / the youth 年輕人 / the public 公眾
- the aristocracy 貴族 / the bourgeoisie 資產階級 /
  the proletariat 普羅大眾 / the working class 工人階級 /
  the middle class 中產人士
- the majority 多數 / the minority 少數
- the government 政府 / the staff 職員 / the audience 觀眾；聽眾 / the jury 陪審團 / the congregation 會眾 / the committee 委員會 / the crowd 人群 / the crew 機組人員 / the mob 群氓
- He vanished into the crowd. 他消失在人群中。
- She was invited to join the staff of TVB.
  她受聘在無線電視台任職。

## ⚡ 5.2 用法速查表
**Speed check**

### 定冠詞與特指的群體：

| 場合 | 例子 |
| --- | --- |
| **A** 定冠詞 + 單數可數名詞<br>the + singular countable noun | The crocodile is very dangerous. 鱷魚是非常危險的。 |
| **B** 定冠詞 + 複數名詞<br>the + plural noun | the bosses 老闆們 / the workers 工人們 |
| **C** 定冠詞 + 形容詞<br>the + adjective | the sick 患者 / the rich 富人 |
| **D** 定冠詞 + 集合名詞<br>the + collective noun | the public 公眾 / the crowd 人群 /<br>the middle class 中產人士 |

# 06 DEFINITE ARTICLE *THE* AND PROPER NOUNS
## 定冠詞 THE 與專有名詞的關係

**一般來講,專有名詞前面不用定冠詞,但以下情況則屬例外。**

## 6.1 怎樣用
### Usage

用途

**A** the + 姓氏。

用在姓氏的複數名詞之前,表示"一家人,或這一姓的夫婦二人"。

- the Obamas 奧巴馬家族 / the Pengs 彭氏一家
- The Lins live upstairs. 林氏夫婦住在樓上。
- The Johns are watching TV. 約翰一家在看電視。

☞ 比較 11 A 人名

用途

# B the + 複數名稱。

以複數形式表示的群體 ( 如家族、種族、團隊 )，可被看作是整體的一群。

例

（家庭成員）

- The Zhang brothers have opened a bakery.
  張氏兄弟開設了一家麵包店。

（種族）

- How did the Europeans treat the Native Americans when they first came into the new world?
  歐洲人來到美洲新大陸時，他們如何對待當地的原居民？

（球隊）

- The Chicago Bulls 芝加哥公牛隊 / The New York Yankees 紐約洋基隊

（政治）

- In the Legco election, the Pan-democrats secured a total of 27 seats.
  在立法會選舉中，泛民合共取得 27 個議席。
- The Liberals were the main political threat to the Conservatives.
  自由黨是保守黨的主要政敵。

**用途 C the + 國籍名稱。**

一些以 -sh、-ch、-ese、-ss 結尾的國籍名稱，屬於不可數名詞，必須加上定冠詞 the 來表示國籍。

- the British 英國人
- the Spanish 西班牙人
- the Swedish 瑞典人
- the Swiss 瑞士人
- the French 法國人
- the Chinese 中國人
- the Burmese 緬甸人
- the Taiwanese 台灣人
- the Japanese 日本人
- the Vietnamese 越南人

※ 注意，在表示國籍的複數可數名詞前用零冠詞。

☞ 9 C 國籍與宗教

**用途 D 國家名稱等。**

當國家名稱、機關團體等出現名詞如 kingdom、republic、union 時，多用定冠詞 the。

- (王國) the United Kingdom 聯合王國 (英國) / the Kingdom of Thailand 泰王國 / the Kingdom of Denmark 丹麥王國
- (共和國) the People's Republic of China 中華人民共和國 / the Republic of Slovenia 斯洛維尼亞共和國
- (聯邦) the United States 美國 / the Commonwealth of Australia 澳大利亞聯邦
- (聯盟) the European Union 歐洲聯盟 / the United Nations 聯合國

☞ 比較 11 B 國家與城市

用途

## 地理名稱。

大多數地名用零冠詞（11 C 地名），但也不盡然，特別是當專有名詞中出現下列可數名詞時，則多用定冠詞 the：

| bay | canal | channel | gulf |
|-----|-------|---------|------|
| ocean | river | sea | strait |

- （海洋）the Pacific Ocean 太平洋 / the Atlantic Ocean 大西洋
- （海）the Yellow Sea 黃海 / the East China Sea 東海
- （海灣）the Persian Gulf 波斯灣 / the Gulf of Mexico 墨西哥灣
- （運河）the Suez Canal 蘇伊士運河 / the Panama Canal 巴拿馬運河
- （海峽）the Taiwan Straits 台灣海峽 / the English Channel 英倫海峽
- （江河）the Nile 尼羅河 / the Tam-Shui River 淡水河 / the Yangtze River 長江 / the Yellow River 黃河 / the Pearl River 珠江
- （湖）the West Lake 西湖 / the Inle Lake 茵萊湖
- （群島）the Okinawa Islands 琉球群島 / the Hawaiian Islands 夏威夷群島 / the British Isles 布列顛群島 / the Galápagos Islands 加拉巴哥群島
- （山脈）the Alps 阿爾卑斯山脈 / the Himalayas 喜瑪拉雅山脈
- （盆地）the Taipei Basin 台北盆地 / the Yellow River Basin 黃河流域 / the Amazon Basin 亞馬遜流域
- （平原）the Great Plains（美國）大平原 / the Jia-Nan Plains 嘉南平原
- （高原）the Tibetan Plateau 西藏高原 / the Persian Plateau 伊朗高原
- （沙漠）the Sahara Desert 撒哈拉沙漠 / the Gobi Desert 戈壁沙漠
- （瀑布）the Niagara Falls 尼亞加拉大瀑布 / the Huangguoshu Falls 黃果樹大瀑布

※ 注意，在地圖上，以上地名中的 the 經常被省略。

☞ 比較 11 C 地名

用途

## 其他獨一無二的事物。

英語許多普通名詞本來沒有甚麼專指性，但加上定冠詞就特指了某些事物，有些再大寫後，就成了專有名詞。在這情況下便需要加上定冠詞。

（名勝古蹟）

- the Great Sphinx 獅身人面像 / the Great Pyramid 金字塔 / the Statue of Liberty 自由女神像 / the Tower of London 倫敦塔 / the Great Wall 長城 / the Summer Palace 頤和園

（建築物）

- the Great Hall of the People 人民大會堂 / the National Chiang Kai-shek Memorial Hall 國立中正紀念堂 / the City Hall 大會堂 / the Space Museum 太空館 / The British Museum 大英博物館

（歷史大事）

- the May Fourth Movement 五四運動 / the October Revolution 十月革命 / the Long March 長征 / the Rizal Park Hostage-taking Incident 馬尼拉人質事件（黎剎公園人質事件）

（政黨）

- the Communist Party 共產黨 / the Pan-Green Coalition 泛綠聯盟 / the Hong Kong Federation of Trade Unions 香港工會聯合會

（公務機構）

- the Legislative Council 立法會 / the Department of Education 教育部 / the Chinese People's Liberation Army 中國人民解放軍

（組織）

- the Boy Scouts 男童軍 / the Red Cross 紅十字會

## 6.2 用法速查表
### Speed check

**定冠詞和專有名詞的關係:**

| 場合 | 例子 |
| --- | --- |
| **A** the + 複數名詞 | the Europeans 歐洲人 / the Pan-democrats 泛民派 |
| **B** the + 國家名稱 | the United Kingdom 英國 / the United States 美國 |
| **C** the + 國籍名稱 | the Chinese 中國人 / the Spanish 西班牙人 |
| **D** the + 姓名 | the Obamas 奧巴馬家族 / the Pengs 彭氏一家 |
| **E** the + 地理名稱 | the Pacific Ocean 太平洋 / the Alps 阿爾卑斯山脈 |
| **F** 其他獨一無二的事物 | the Boy Scouts 男童軍 / The British Museum 大英博物館 |

# 07 DEFINITE ARTICLE *THE* AND TIME
## 定冠詞 THE 與時間的關係

定冠詞與時間的關係相當密切，既可特指某年代或時期，又可指一天的某個時段，還可表示一整段時間，或用在表示時間的關係子句裏。

 ## 7.1 怎樣用
### Usage

 **用途**

## A 表示特定的時期。

在世紀、年代等名詞前用 the。

 **例**
- the Jurassic　侏羅紀時代
- the Prehistoric Time　史前時期
- the Stone Age　石器時代
- the Ming Dynasty　明朝
- the Renaissance　文藝復興時期
- the 1960s　一九六零年代
- the 21st century　二十一世紀

☞ 比較 11 G 節日

用途

**B** **表示較前或較後的時間。**

（與 before 連用表示前天的時間）

- the day before yesterday 前天 / the night before last 前晚
- the day before yesterday in the morning / afternoon / evening
  前天的早上 / 下午 / 傍晚

（與 after 連用表示後天的時間）

- the day after tomorrow 後天 / the night after next 後晚
- the day after tomorrow in the morning / afternoon / evening
  後天的早上 / 下午 / 傍晚

（與 before last 或 after next 連用，表示前後的星期、月份、日子等）

- the Monday / week / month / January / Christmas / century
  before last 上上個星期一 / 星期 / 月 / 一月 / 聖誕節 / 世紀
- the year before last 上年再上年
- the Monday / week / month / January / Christmas / century
  after next 下下個星期一 / 星期 / 月 / 一月 / 聖誕節 / 世紀
- the year after next 下年再下年

（用 the other day / morning 等，指剛剛過去的那一天或那一個早上等）

- I ran into Maggie the other morning. 剛過去的那一個早上我碰見瑪姬。

☞ 比較 11 F 星期、月份、季節等

用途

## 表示一整段時間。

（一日之中的不同時段）

- in the morning / in the afternoon / in the evening 在早上 / 下午 / 傍晚
- in the day 在白天 / in the dusk 日落時份

☞ 比較 12 B 一日中的不同時段

（某特定時期或某一段時間）

- in the holidays 在假期裏
- at the age of 18 在 18 歲時
- in the 1980s 或 in the 1980's 20 世紀 80 年代
- in the 19th century 在 19 世紀

（用 during / throughout the whole / entire ... 以強調過去整段時間內所發生的事）

- It was very cold during the winter. 那年的冬天很冷。
- He was bedridden and sickly throughout the whole winter.
  整個冬天他一直臥病在牀。
- During the entire summer holidays, I never met any friend.
  整個暑假我一個朋友都沒有見過。

☞ 比較 11 F 星期、月份、季節等

用途

## 表示時間的順序。

- the present / the past / the future 現在 / 過去 / 未來
- the beginning 開始：at the beginning of the month 在月初
- the middle 中間：I'm in the middle of lunch. 我正在吃午飯。
- the end 最後：I started work at the end of June.
  我是在六月底開始工作的。
- the first 起初：I knew from the (very) first it would never
  succeed. 從一開始我就知道這絕不會成功。
- the last 最後：I've been here for the last week. 最近一星期我
  一直在這裏。/ That's the last time I invite her to dinner. 那是我
  最後一次請她吃晚飯。
- the next 下次的；緊接着來到的：Where will you be during
  the next few weeks? 接下來的幾個星期你在哪裏？
- the next morning / day 第二天早上：He rang me and we
  arranged to meet the next day. 他給我打電話，我們安排次日
  見面。

用途

## 用在表示時間的關係子句裏。

定冠詞用在表示時間的 relative clause（關係子句）裏。

- 1997 was the year when Hong Kong was returned to China.
  1997 那一年，香港回歸中國。
- The summer of 1997, when Hong Kong was returned to China,
  will never be forgotten.
  大家不會忘記 1997 年的夏天，那時香港回歸中國。
- I still remember the summer that we went on a tour to Europe.
  我還記得那年夏天我們去了歐洲旅行。

☞ 比較 8 F 定冠詞 + 關係子句

## 7.2 用法速查表
### Speed check

**定冠詞用於表示時間：**

| 場合 | 例子 |
| --- | --- |
| A 表示特定時間 | the Triassic 三疊紀時代 /<br>the Ming Dynasty 明朝 |
| B 表示較前或較後時間 | the day before yesterday 前天 /<br>the night before last 前晚<br>the day after tomorrow 後天 /<br>the night after next 後晚 |
| C 表示整段時間 | in the morning 在早上 / in the afternoon 下午 /<br>in the evening 傍晚<br>It was very cold during the winter. 那年冬季很冷。 |
| D 表示時間順序 | the beginning 開始 / the middle 中間 /<br>the end 最後 |
| E 用在表示時間的關係子句裏 | 1997 was the year when Hong Kong was returned to China.<br>1997 那一年，香港回歸中國。 |

# 08 DEFINITE ARTICLE *THE* : OTHER GRAMMATICAL FUNCTIONS

## 定冠詞 THE 的其他語法功能

定冠詞必然有明確所指，在文法上，它與不同的語法項目配合會產生不同意義。

### 8.1 怎樣用
#### Usage

**用途**

**A** 定冠詞 + 形容詞最高級。

在 the superlative（形容詞最高級）前用定冠詞，專指某東西。

- the strongest man / the widest river / the ugliest dog
  最強壯的男人 / 最寬闊的河流 / 最醜陋的狗
- the most beautiful woman / the most expensive car
  最漂亮的女人 / 最昂貴的車
- Mirror, mirror on the wall. Who is the fairest of them all?
  魔鏡魔鏡告訴我，最美的女人是我麼？
- Burj Khalifa in Dubai is the tallest building in the world.
  全球最高的大廈是位於杜拜的哈利法塔。

## 用途 B 表示兩者間的比較。

表示兩者間 "較……的一個" 時用定冠詞。

- He is the stronger of the two boys.
  兩個男孩之中,他是較強壯的那個。
- The taller of the two prisoners killed the policeman.
  兩個囚犯之中,個子高些的那個殺了警員。

## 用途 C the + 序數詞。

用在 ordinal number (序數詞) 或表示序列的 next、last 等前,以專指某東西。

例
- I live on the fiftieth floor. 我住在 50 樓。
- She was the first woman to win this coveted prize.
  她是第一位女性贏得這個人人夢寐以求的獎項。
- This may be the last chance. 這可能是最後一次機會。
- Let's catch the next train. 我們趕下一班車吧。

※ 注意,在以下情況裏,序數詞前不用定冠詞。
(1) 序數詞前有物主代詞:my first smartphone / his second car
(2) 序數詞作副詞:He came first in the race.
(3) 在固定片語中:at first / first of all / from first to last

※ 注意,序數詞表示 "又一" 時,前面用不定冠詞 a / an。

- He bought a second pair of jeans. 他又買了一條牛仔褲。
- He ate a hamburger, then a second, then a third...
  他吃了一個漢堡包,又吃了第二個,又吃了第三個……

用途 **D** the + only / very / same。

定冠詞用於形容詞 only、very、same 等前面,表示獨特、唯一的東西。

- The Only Love (Bee Gees) 唯一的戀愛(歌名)
- The Very Thought of You (Nat King Cole) 我是真的想你(歌名)
- That's the very thing I've been looking for.
  那正是我要找的東西。
- The only thing I want is for you to be happy, whether it be with me or without me.
  我唯一希望的只是你能快樂,無論有我在還是沒有。
- The two boys are of the same height. 兩個男孩的身高相等。

用途 **E** the + 名詞 + of。

定冠詞與 of 連用以特指有關的論題。

- the editor of this book 這本書的編輯
- The Voice of China 中國好聲音
- the culprits of food-safety scandals 食物安全醜聞的元兇
- the sources of widespread public discontent
  社會上普遍存在的不滿情緒的根源
- the popularity of South Korean culture 韓風之盛行
- the Chief Executive of HKSAR
  香港特別行政區行政長官(香港特首)
- the secret history of aliens on Earth 外星人在地球上的秘史
- Thailand is about the size of France. 泰國與法國的面積相若。
- Vienna is known as the city of music. 維也納被譽為音樂之都。

用途

## 定冠詞 + 關係子句。

某些關係子句必須使用定冠詞。

- They are the men who I met yesterday.
  他們就是我昨天遇到的那幾個人。
- She is the girl whose iPhone was stolen.
  她就是 iPhone 被偷了的那個女孩。
- This is the place where I grew up.
  這是我長大的地方。
- These are the pineapple cakes that I bought in Taipei.
  這是我在台北買的鳳梨酥。
- These are the beggars to whom I gave the money.
  他們就是我給了錢的乞丐。
- It is the only toilet which is made entirely of gold.
  這是唯一一座用黃金製造的廁所。
- That is the reason why I dislike her.
  這就是我不喜歡她的原因。

用途

## 用在慣用語中的定冠詞。

某些慣用語必須使用定冠詞。

- at the top：At the top of the hill stood the tiny chapel.
  那座小教堂矗立在山頂上。
- at the end of the day 最終；到頭來：At the end of the day you
  will have to decide which subjects you want to take. 你最終要
  決定自己要選修哪幾科。
- by the way 順便說：順便說一下：By the way, what time is it?
  順便問一下，現在幾點？
- in the distance：In the distance could be seen the snow mountains.
  遠處可以見到雪山。
- in the sky / in the dark / in the rain 在天空上 / 在黑暗中 / 在雨
  中：Singin' in the Rain is a famous American musical comedy.
  《萬花嬉春》是一齣著名的美國音樂劇喜劇。

- on the whole 一般來說；大體上：On the whole she is a very difficult woman. 總的來說她是個很難對付的女人。
- on the way 在⋯⋯路上：Guess who I bumped in to on the way home? 猜猜我在回家的路上碰到了誰？
- on the phone：He told me on the phone about the accident. 他在電話裏告訴了我這宗意外。

## 8.2 用法速查表
### Speed check

| 定冠詞的其他語法功能： | |
| --- | --- |
| 場合 | 例子 |
| **A** 定冠詞 + 形容詞最高級 | the strongest woman |
| **B** 表示兩者間的比較 | the younger of the two girls |
| **C** 定冠詞 + 序數詞 | the second son |
| **D** 定冠詞 + only / very / same | the only love / the very thought of you / of the same height |
| **E** 定冠詞 + 名詞 + of | The Voice of China / the city of music |
| **F** 用在關係字句中 | That is the reason why I dislike her. |
| **G** 用在慣用語中 | by the way / at the end of the day |

# 09 ZERO ARTICLE + PLURAL COUNTABLE NOUNS
# 零冠詞 + 複數可數名詞

通常我們在三類名詞前不帶冠詞：複數可數名詞、不可數名詞和專有名詞。此節討論零冠詞和複數可數名詞的關係，在一般敘述的情況下，在說明人、地點、食物、職業、國籍、動物、植物等情況時，其前面用零冠詞。

 ## 9.1 怎樣用
### Usage

用途

**A** 一類人。

在表示一類人的複數可數名詞前用零冠詞。

- Not all ø boys like ball games. 不是所有男孩都喜歡球類遊戲。
- Why do ø girls always want to be slim?
  為甚麼女孩總是喜歡瘦身？
- This TV programme is not suitable for ø children.
  這電視節目不適合兒童觀看。

用途

 **B**

## 職業。

在表示一類職業的複數可數名詞前用零冠詞。

- Both my mother and father are ø teachers. 我父母同是教師。
- What do ø astrophysicists do? 天體物理學家的工作是甚麼？
- ø Hospital nurses usually work in shifts.
  醫院護士通常要輪流值班工作。

用途

 **C**

## 國籍與宗教。

在表示國籍的複數可數名詞前用零冠詞。

- ø Indians believe in many religions. 印度人有許多宗教信仰。
- ø Buddhists are vegetarians. 佛教徒是素食者。
- More and more ø Italians are leaving their country because they cannot get a job.
  越來越多意大利人因為無法找到工作而離鄉別井。
- ø African Americans are twice as likely to die from stroke as ø Caucasians.
  美籍黑人因中風死亡的比率比白種人高出一倍。

※ 注意，一些以 -ch、-sh、-ese 結尾來表示國籍的名詞則屬例外，這些名詞不可數，必須加上定冠詞 the 來表示國籍，例如 the French（法國人）、the Spanish（西班牙人）、the Chinese（中國人）、the British（英國人）。

☞ 6 C 國籍名稱

用途

## 動植物。

在表示一類動物的複數可數名詞前用零冠詞。

例
- ø Dogs are faithful animals. 狗是忠心的動物。
- ø Sharks don't usually attack humans. 鯊魚一般不會襲擊人類。
- ø Oxen are quiet and unassuming animals that give back far more than they take.
  牛是平和謙遜的動物，只管付出，不問回報。

也適用於表示植物的複數可數名詞前。

例
- We use ø roses for many purposes. 玫瑰有多方面的用途。
- ø Trees lose their leaves in winter. 樹木在冬天落葉。

用途

## 地點。

在表示地點或場所的複數可數名詞前用零冠詞。

- This is a list of ø hospitals and other medical facilities in Hong Kong. 此名單列出香港醫院和其他醫療設備場所。
- ø Museums are closed on Tuesdays. 星期二博物館關門。
- Can eBooks and ø libraries coexist?
  電子書和圖書館可以並存嗎？

用途

## 產品或機器。

在表示產品與機器的複數可數名詞前用零冠詞。

- ø iPads have become very popular. iPads 變得很流行。
- These cars are built by ø robots. 這些汽車用機械人製造。
- What else will ø smartphones replace, in part or whole?
  智慧型電話將來還會部份或完全取代其他甚麼東西嗎？

# 9.2 用法速查表
### Speed check

| 零冠詞 + 複數可數名詞: | |
| --- | --- |
| **場合** | **例子** |
| **A** 一類人 | ø Boys like playing ball games. |
| **B** 職業 | ø Social workers are helpful people. |
| **C** 國籍與宗教 | ø Muslims don't like pork. |
| **D** 動植物 | ø Dogs are faithful animals. |
| **E** 地點 | ø Museums are closed on Tuesdays. |
| **F** 產品或機器 | ø iPads have become very popular. |

# 10

# ZERO ARTICLE + UNCOUNTABLE NOUNS
# 零冠詞 + 不可數名詞

此節討論零冠詞與不可數名詞的關係。在不可數名詞（總是單數）前使用零冠詞是個常見做法，在一般敘述的情況下，在說明食物、材料、顏色、運動、行為等情況時，其前面都用零冠詞。

## 10.1 怎樣用
### Usage

**用途**

**A** 食物與飲料。

在表示食物與飲料的不可數名詞前用零冠詞。

**例**
- Do you take Ø sugar in your coffee? 你喝咖啡加糖嗎？
- Making Ø sushi at home is fun! 在家裏自製壽司很好玩啊！
- Ø Rice doesn't grow in northern China, which is much drier and colder.
  稻米不在中國北方生長，那裏氣候比較乾燥寒冷。

※ 注意，只有特指時才加定冠詞 the。比較以下兩例：
- Ø Water boils at 100 °C. 水在攝氏 100 度沸騰。
- The water in this river is polluted. 這條河的水已受到污染。

用途

## 物質與材料。

在表示物質與材料的不可數名詞前不用冠詞。

- The desk is made of Ø wood. 這桌子是木造的。
- The gate is made of Ø iron. 這道閘門是鐵造的。
- This bread is made from Ø wheat. 這麵包是小麥做的。
- Ø Cotton feels soft. 棉花摸起來柔軟。

※ 注意，只有特指時才加定冠詞 the。比較以下兩例：
- Every year, large amounts of Ø plastics enter the sea.
  每年都有大量的塑膠流入海洋。
- Once in the sea, the plastics biodegrade extremely slowly.
  一旦進入海洋，這些塑膠只能以極度緩慢的過程進行生物降解。

用途

## 顏色。

在表示顏色的名詞前用零冠詞。

- My favourite colour is ø white. 我最喜歡的顏色是白色。
- Ø Red means danger. 紅色意味危險。
- You mix Ø yellow and Ø blue to make Ø green. 黃加藍變綠。
- Everybody was dressed in Ø black today. 今天大家都穿上黑衣。

**用途 D**

## 運動與遊戲。

運動項目、棋類等名稱前不用冠詞。

- I like ø swimming. 我喜歡游泳。
- He often plays ø basketball on Sunday.
  他很多時候會在星期天踢足球。
- Ø Yoga has become very popular around the world.
  瑜珈在世界各地都很流行。
- Sai Kung is a popular place for Ø hiking. 西貢是遠足的好地方。
- They meet fairly often to play Ø chess.
  他們經常一起下國際象棋。
- The second day events are Ø 110 m hurdles, Ø discus throw, Ø javelin and Ø 1,500 m.
  第二天的比賽項目包括百一米跨欄、擲鐵餅、標槍和千五米長跑。

※ 注意，當球類指具體事物時應加上冠詞。比較以下兩例：
- Let's play Ø football next Saturday. 我們下星期六去踢球吧。
- Where is the football? 足球在哪裏？

**用途 E**

## 行為與習慣。

表示行為與習慣的 gerund（動名詞）前用零冠詞。

- Ø Smoking is bad for our health. 吸煙有害健康。
- Ø Swimming is great exercise. 游泳是很好的鍛煉。
- Don't be afraid of Ø giving. You can never give too much, if you're giving willingly.
  不要害怕付出。真心真意付出的人，永遠不會計較太多。

**用途**

## F 語言與學科。

語言與學科名稱前不用冠詞。

**例**
- Do you like Ø Maths? 你喜歡數學嗎？
- They are communicating in Ø English. 他們以英語溝通。
- Are you studying Ø Spanish? 你在學習西班牙語嗎？

※ 注意，在表示語言的短語中有 language 時，須用定冠詞。
- He is learning the French language. 他正在學習法語。

※ 注意，只有特指時才加定冠詞 the。比較以下兩例：
- She is fond of Ø music. 她對音樂很有興趣。
- The music of the film is wonderful. 這部電影的音樂很動聽。

**用途**

## G 疾病。

疾病名稱前用零冠詞。

**例**
- She has Ø cancer. 她患癌。
- Ø Pneumonia nearly killed him. 肺炎差點奪去他的生命。
- The old man was dying of Ø tuberculosis. 這名老翁死於肺癆。
- The baby has got Ø measles. 那嬰孩在出麻疹。

※ 注意，有些疾病名稱以單數可數名詞標識，一般與不定冠詞連用。
- She caught a cold at school. 她在學校染了感冒。
- I've got a splitting headache. 我頭痛得像要裂開一樣。

☞ 另見 2.1 F 表示病痛

## 用途 H

### 抽象名詞。

抽象名詞是性質、狀態、動作、概念等的名稱，這些名詞一般無複數形式，不加冠詞，例子多不勝數，例如：time（時間）、hope（希望）、friendship（友誼）、knowledge（知識）等等。

- Don't talk Ø nonsense. 不要胡說八道。
- Ø Time is money. 時間就是金錢。
- Ø Beauty is in the heart of the beholder. 情人眼中出西施。
- Ø Equality and Ø freedom have both been identified as important characteristics of Ø democracy.
  平等與自由乃公認為民主之重要特徵。
- Ø Swimming is great exercise. 游泳是很好的鍛煉。
- Spread Ø love everywhere you go. Let no one ever come to you without leaving happier. (Mother Teresa)
  把愛散播至你到過的每處地方，讓與你交會過的人無不歡喜而去。（德蘭修女）

※ 注意，只有特指時才加定冠詞 the。

- The friendship between us is long and lasting.
  我們的友誼天長地久。
- We never know the love of a parent until we become parents ourselves.
  我們要當自己成為父母的時候，才會真正了解何謂父愛或母愛。

## 10.2 用法速查表
### Speed check

**零冠詞 + 不可數名詞：**

| 場合 | 例子 |
|------|------|
| **A** 食物與飲料 | Do you take Ø sugar in your coffee? 你喝咖啡加糖嗎？ |
| **B** 物質與材料 | The desk is made of Ø wood. 這桌子是木造的。 |
| **C** 顏色 | Ø Red means danger. 紅色意味危險。 |
| **D** 運動與遊戲 | Let's have a game of ø chess. 我們兩人下盤棋吧。 |
| **E** 行為與習慣 | Ø Smoking is bad for our health. 吸煙有害健康。 |
| **F** 語言與學科 | He can speak Ø Korean. 他會說韓語。 |
| **G** 疾病 | She has Ø cancer. 她患癌。 |
| **H** 抽象名詞 | Ø Knowledge is Ø power. 知識就是力量。 |

# 11 ZERO ARTICLE + PROPER NOUNS
## 零冠詞 + 專有名詞

專有名詞是特定的某人、某地方或機構的名稱，即：人名、地名、國家名、單位名及組織名等等。專有名詞一般無需確認，所以通常使用零冠詞。

 ## 11.1 怎樣用
### Usage

用途

**A** 人名。

例
- All his life Ø Einstein was trying to understand the laws of the Universe.
  愛恩斯坦終其一生都在鑽研宇宙的規律。
- Ø Lu Xun is known as the Father of Modern Chinese Literature.
  魯迅被稱為中國現代文學之父。

也適用於一般人的名稱。

- Ø Xiao Wang just called in sick. 小王剛打電話回來請病假。
- My best friend is Ø Chloe. 我最要好的朋友是傲兒。

☞ 另見 2.1 D 代表一類人或事物。

用途

### 國家與城市。

國名或城市名稱前用零冠詞。

- Ø China 中國 / Ø America 美國 / Ø Canada 加拿大
- Ø Beijing 北京 / Ø Seoul 首爾 / Ø Bangkok 曼谷
- Ø London is the capital of Ø England. 倫敦是英國的首都。
- Ø China is the world's most populous country.
  中國是世界上人口最多的國家。

※ 注意，組合國名、縮寫國名或以群島組成的國名則屬例外，必須加上定冠詞。

- the United States 美國
- the U.K. 英國
- the Philippines 菲律賓
- the Penghu Islands 澎湖列島

☞ 另見 6 D 國家名稱

**用途**

# C 地名。

地名都是唯一的，在形式上用大寫，不需要用冠詞。

- （大陸）Asia 亞洲 / Europe 歐洲 / Australia 澳洲 /
  Africa 非洲 / America 美洲
- （地域）Outer Mongolia 外蒙古 / Guangzhou 廣州 /
  California 加州
- （島嶼）Easter Island 復活島 / Lantau Island 大嶼山 /
  Green Island 綠島
- （海港）Victoria Harbour 維多利亞港 / Port Jackson 傑克遜港
- （山峰）Mount Everest 珠穆朗瑪峰（額菲爾士峰）/
  Mount A-Li 阿里山 / Mount Fuji 富士山 / Mount Parker 柏架山
- （湖泊）Sun Moon Lake 日月潭 / West Lake 西湖 /
  Lake Michigan 密西根湖 / Plover Cove Reservoir 船灣淡水湖
- （城市）Shanghai 上海 / New York 紐約 / Shenzhen 深圳
- （公園）Ocean Park 海洋公園 / Yellow Stone National Park
  黃石公園
- （街道）Nan Jing East Road 南京東路 / Tenth Avenue
  第十大道 / Nathan Road 彌敦道 / 北部橫貫公路 Northern
  Cross Island Highway
- （機場）Narita Airport 成田空港 / Songshan Airport 松山機場
- （車站）Kowloon Station 九龍站 / Taipei Railway Station 台北
  火車站

☞ 比較 6 E 地名

## 用途 D

# 職位或頭銜。

在表示稱號、職位、頭銜、身份等名詞前不加冠詞。

- Ø Mr / Miss / Ms / Mrs Lu 陸先生 / 小姐 / 女士 / 太太
- Ø Dr Thompson 湯普生醫生
- Ø Professor Wang 王教授
- Ø President Lincoln 林肯總統
- Ø Dean of the English Department 英語系主任
- He is Ø chairman of the Students' Union. 他是學生會主席。

※ 注意，以上職位大體是指獨一的職位，"主席"、"主任"都只有一個，如不是獨一的要加不定冠詞。

- She is a professor in the English Department.
  她是英語系的一名教授。

## 用途 E

# 星期、月份、季節等。

時間（星期、月份、四季、年份）前用零冠詞。

- We have no classes on Ø Saturday. 星期六我們不用上課。
- The new school year begins in Ø September. 新學年在九月開始。
- In Ø autumn, we like to go camping. 我們喜歡在秋天去露營。

※ 注意，秋天的美式說法是 fall，前面須加 the，即 in the fall (= in autumn)。

※ 注意，只有特指時才加定冠詞 the。

- It was very hot during the summer. 那年夏天很熱。
- During the whole winter he never saw a soul.
  在整個冬天他沒見過一個人。

**節日名稱。**

在喜慶節日名稱前用零冠詞。

- They always go to church at Ø Easter.
  他們在復活節時總是去教堂。
- We plan to go skiing in Hokkaido at Ø Christmas.
  我們計劃在聖誕節時去北海道滑雪。
- Most fancy dress parties are held around Ø Halloween.
  大部份的化粧舞會都會在萬聖節期間舉行。
- Some people don't feel like celebrating Ø Valentine's Day.
  有些人不喜歡慶祝情人節。

※ 注意，某些中國傳統節日除外。

- the Spring Festival  春節
- the Mid-Autumn Festival  中秋節

# 11.2 用法速查表
## Speed check

**零冠詞 + 專有名詞:**

| 場合 | 例子 |
| --- | --- |
| **A** 人名 | Ø Einstein was a very famous scientist.<br>愛恩斯坦是個大名鼎鼎的科學家。 |
| **B** 國家名 | Ø London is the capital of Ø England.<br>倫敦是英國的首都。 |
| **C** 地名 | Ø Europe 歐洲 / Ø Guangzhou 廣州 /<br>Ø Lantau Island 大嶼山 |
| **D** 職位或頭銜 | Ø Mr / Miss / Ms / Mrs Lu 陸先生 / 小姐 / 女士 / 太太<br>Ø Dr Thompson 湯普遜醫生 |
| **E** 星期、月份、季節等 | on Ø Saturday 在星期六<br>in Ø September 在九月<br>in Ø autumn 在秋天 |
| **F** 節日名稱 | at Ø Easter 在復活節時<br>at Ø Christmas 在聖誕節時 |

# 12 ZERO ARTICLE: SPECIAL USAGE
## 零冠詞的特殊用法

---

 12.1 怎樣用
### Usage

用途

**A** 家庭成員之間的稱呼。

在日常會話中，家庭成員之間的稱呼不用加冠詞。

- Thank you, Uncle / Auntie. 謝謝你，叔叔 / 阿姨。
- What time will Ø Father be home? 爸爸甚麼時候回家？
- Ø Mum's gone to market. 媽媽去菜市場了。
- Ø Grandpa goes for a walk in the park every morning.
  爺爺每天早上去公園散步。
- Hey Ø Sis, can I do anything to help?
  哎，姐姐，我能幫甚麼忙嗎？

可單獨使用來表示親屬關係的稱呼還有：

- Mother / Mum ( 英式 ) / Mummy ( 英式 ) / Mom ( 美式 ) /
  Mommy ( 美式 )
- Father / Daddy / Dad / Pa / Pop ( 美式 )
- Granddad / Grandpa / Grandma

用途

# 一日之內的不同時段。

某些表示一日之內的時間的名詞前用零冠詞。

- from Ø morning till Ø night 從早到晚
- from Ø dawn to Ø dusk 從黎明到黃昏
- We got up before Ø sunrise. 我們在日出前就起牀了。
- The farmers finish work at Ø sunset. 農夫日入而息。

類似例子還包括：

- at Ø daybreak 破曉時份
- around Ø noon 接近中午
- by Ø midnight 到午夜之前
- before Ø daylight 天還未亮時

※ 注意，某些表示時間的固定片語（如 in the morning 早上 / in the afternoon 下午 / in the evening 傍晚）則屬例外。

☞ 比較 7 A 一日中的不同時段或日子

用途

# 餐飲名稱。

三餐飯菜的名詞前用零冠詞。

- I usually have Ø breakfast at seven o'clock.
  我通常七點吃早餐。
- What would you like for Ø lunch? 你午餐喜歡吃些甚麼？
- Are we expected to dress for Ø dinner? 我們應該穿禮服赴宴嗎？

也適用於早午餐 (brunch) 或傍晚茶點 (high tea) 等。

- We had afternoon tea at Shangri-La.
  我們在香格里拉酒店喝下午茶。

※ 注意，三餐飯前帶有形容詞修飾時，應加不定冠詞。

- I had a quick breakfast at McDonald.
  我匆匆地在麥當勞吃了早餐。
- We had a very nice lunch yesterday.
  我們昨天吃了個很不錯的午餐。

※ 注意，在具體指某頓飯時要加定冠詞。

- The brunch I ordered still hasn't arrived.
  我要的早午餐還沒有來。

**D 交通工具。**

用 "by + 名詞" 表示交通工具的時候，該名詞前用零冠詞。

- to travel by Ø car / train 乘汽車 / 火車旅行
- It is about 10 minutes away by Ø bus.
  離這裏大概是十分鐘巴士車程那麼遠。

常見的這類例子還有：

- by bike 騎自行車
- by taxi 乘計程車
- by ship 乘船
- by plane 乘飛機

可引伸指旅行或郵件寄遞方式。

- It is quicker by Ø air than by Ø sea. 乘坐飛機比坐輪船快。
- Send this parcel by Ø air mail. 用航空郵件寄出這包裹。

※ 注意，如不用 "by + 名詞" 這結構則要在名詞前加定冠詞。比較以下兩例：

- We'll go by Ø train. 我們會坐火車去。
- We'll take the train. 我們會乘坐火車。

用途

## 不具體的處所。

當 church、school、market、hospital、college、university 等表示"處所"的名詞所指的不是具體地點時,前面通常用零冠詞。

例
- go to Ø market  去市場
- in Ø hospital  住院(治療)
- in Ø jail  服刑
- They go to Ø church every Sunday.  他們每個星期天去做禮拜。
- She goes to Ø school on foot.  她步行上學。
- He was greatly disappointed when he didn't get into Ø university.
  沒能考上大學,他當時極為沮喪。

常見的這類名詞還有 bed、class、sea、home、town、prison 等。

- at Ø home 在家裏
- I go to Ø bed at 10:30. 我十點半上牀睡覺。

※ 注意,如果是指明地點,其前面就要加上冠詞。
- Don't go to the bed. 不要到牀前去。
- There is a prison in Stanley. 赤柱那裏有一所監獄。

用途

## 成對事物。

零冠詞用於以 and 連接的成對事物。

例
- Ø day and night 日夜
- Ø father and son 父子
- Ø light and dark 光明與黑暗
- Ø sun and moon 日月
- Grimm tales for Ø young and old 老幼皆宜的格林童話
- learn how to draw in Ø pen and ink 學習用筆墨繪畫
- This cafeteria is run by Ø husband and wife.
  這家小餐館由一對夫婦經營。

☞ 比較 2 H 自然成對的名詞

用途

## 量詞之後的名詞。

量詞之後的名詞,不管是可數或不可數名詞,通常用零冠詞。

例 (不可數名詞)

- a cup of Ø tea 一杯茶
- a slice of Ø bread 一片麵包
- a bar of Ø chocolate 一塊朱古力
- a round of Ø applause 一片掌聲
- a bottle of Ø wine 一瓶葡萄酒
- a barrel of Ø beer 一桶啤酒
- a piece of Ø paper 一張紙

例 (可數名詞)

- a pair of Ø shoes 一雙鞋子
- a pride of Ø lions 一群獅子
- a mob of Ø rioters 一群示威者

此外,用在 (a) kind of / sort of / type of... 等表示類屬的短語之後的名詞,不論是可數或不可數,也不加冠詞。

- It's a kind of Ø snake. 這是蛇類的一種。
- I'm a type of Ø doctor. 我可以說是一類醫生。
- He is the kind of Ø person who is always late.
  他是那種總會遲到的人。

## 固定短語。

英語有不少約定俗成的慣用語都會用零冠詞。

- for Ø example 例如：I know many young people who can speak Korean – Fred for Ø example.
  我知道有很多年青人會講韓語，費雷德就是其中之一。
- by Ø hand 手工的：This book is written by Ø hand, not typed or printed.
  這本書是手寫的，不是打字或印刷本。
- by Ø machine 用機器：Drawing isn't something that can be done by Ø machine.
  繪畫並不是機器能做到的事情。
- in Ø trouble 陷入困境：The girl was in Ø trouble so I swam out to save her.
  這女孩處於險境，所以我游過去救她。
- in Ø charge of 負責：Students should not be left alone in Ø charge of the school laboratory.
  不應當讓學生單獨管理學校的實驗室。
- in Ø danger 處於危險中：The patient's life is in Ø danger.
  病人生命垂危。
- in Ø fact 實際上：I don't like her; in Ø fact, I hate her.
  我並不喜歡她，事實上我討厭她。
- catch Ø fire 着火：The boxes couldn't catch Ø fire by themselves.
  這些盒子自己不會着火。
- set Ø fire to 放火燒：Someone must have set Ø fire to them deliberately.
  必定有人故意縱火。

# 12.2 用法速查表
## Speed check

**零冠詞的特殊用法：**

| 場合 | 例子 |
| --- | --- |
| **A** 家庭成員之間的稱呼 | Ø Mum's gone to market. 媽媽去菜市場了。 |
| **B** 一日內的不同時段 | We got up before Ø sunrise. 我們在日出前就起淋了。 |
| **C** 餐飲名稱 | What would you like for Ø lunch?<br>你午餐喜歡吃些甚麼？ |
| **D** 交通工具 | to travel by Ø car / train 乘汽車 / 火車旅行 |
| **E** 不具體的處所 | at Ø home 在家裏<br>in Ø hospital 住院（治療） |
| **F** 成對事物 | Ø day and night 日夜<br>Ø father and son 父子 |
| **G** 量詞之後的名詞 | a cup of Ø tea 一杯茶<br>a slice of Ø bread 一片麵包 |
| **H** 固定短語 | for Ø example 例如<br>in Ø charge of 負責<br>in Ø fact 實際上 |

# Section 2: Integrated Sentence Exercises

 綜合句子練習

I 填空題（在橫線上填上 a、an、the 或 ∅）。

1 Jason is _____ interesting person.

2 Colin ate _____ piece of apple pie.

3 We always have _____ breakfast at 8 o'clock.

4 He walks ten miles _____ hour.

5 The children have gone to _____ school.

6 _____ Friday is casual wear day.

7 I do not like _____ football.

8 He will be back in _____ day or two.

9 He is in _____ prison.

10 She is in _____ red.

11 I looked up and saw _____ UFO.

12 Is _____ nuclear energy safe?

13 _____ Dinosaurs / _____ dinosaurs do not exist now.

14 What is _____ proper attire for casual Fridays?

15 _____ policewoman is waiting for you downstairs.

16 I was never very good at _____ maths.

17 Juliet is not allowed to associate with Romeo because he is _____ Montague.

18 Josephine often made _____ unwise decisions.

19 What _____ interesting person!

20 Do you usually have _____cream in your coffee?

21 Someone is knocking at _____ door. Can you answer it?

22 John is talking to his girlfriend on _____ phone.

23 He's in _____class.

24 He went to _____ prison for tax evasion.

25 The monkeys are picking _____ coconuts.

26 Irina can play _____ violin.

27 He comes from _____ far north.

28 We are driving _____south.

29 _____ number of friends came to my birthday party.

30 I'm afraid you've got _____ wrong number.

31 We drive round _____ city.

32 What foods do _____babies like best?

33 I think _____ woman over there is very unfriendly.

34 ICC is _____ tallest building in Hong Kong.

35 I expect it will rain in _____ afternoon.

36 We travelled mostly by _____ night.

37 Tom and David were playing _____ table tennis.

38 She is preparing _____ dinner by herself.

39 _____Chocolate / _____ chocolate makes you fat.

40 She is _____ only person who knows my secret.

41 She's phoned five times during _____ last half hour.

42 My old school is giving _____ fund raising dinner.

43 It never snows here in _____ winter.

44 In _____ charity there is no excess.

45 He would devote his whole life to _____ environmental protection.

46 We'll be there around _____ midnight.

47 You can't borrow my tablet. It's _____ only one I've got.

48 _____ Happiness / _____ happiness multiplies as we divide it with others.

49 Carrying _____ luxury bag, Lulu feels very proud of herself.

50 Does she wear _____ uniform?

II 根據提示，翻譯以下句子。

1 樹木在南極不能生長。

   _____ Antarctic.

2 這些是我僅有的鑰匙。

   These keys are _____ I've got.

3 我買了一套漂亮的杯碟。

   I bought _____ .

4 他因縱火罪而入獄。

   He _____ for arson.

5 有個警員在門口等你。

   _____ is waiting for you at the door.

6 我喉嚨痛。

   _____ sore throat.

7 我哥哥是建築師。

   My brother _____ .

8　設計這座橋的那位建築師獲了獎。

　　_____ won a prize.

9　一位姓朱的先生給您留了言。

　　_____ left a message for you.

10　香港的博物館每逢星期二閉館。

　　_____ in Hong Kong are closed _____.

III 改正以下句子。

1 A knowledge is power.

2 Irina can play violin.

3 Patrick loves reading the novels.

4 They are playing the table tennis.

5 I read a amazing story yesterday.

6 Pandas in Ocean Park are well looked after.

7 My sister does not eat a chicken.

8 I would like piece of cake.

9 The tigers are very rare now.

10 Colin travelled to Philippines.

11 A night is quiet. Let' s take walk!

12 It's a worst play I' ve ever seen.

13 The honesty is best policy.

14 We travelled all over Taipei by the bus.

15 We got up at the dawn to climb to the summit.

16 Spring Festival is time for the family reunions.

17 SOS is a internationally recognized distress call.

18 That is a problem I told you about.

19 A price of gas keeps rising.

20 Chloe can speak the Spanish.

IV 填空題（在橫線上填入 a、an、the 或 ∅）。

1 _____ plane is _____ machine that can fly.

2 She became _____ school teacher after _____ graduation.

3 He is _____ model and _____ artist.

4 I use _____ PC at _____ home.

5 _____ tulip is _____ flower.

6 Tina is _____ engineer. She is also _____ mother.

7 I saw _____ movie_____ last night.

8 They are staying at _____ hotel near _____ Chonburi.

9 They elected him _____ president of _____ U.S.

10 I bought _____ pair of _____ jeans.

11 He found _____ dead man lying on _____ floor.

12 _____ leaves start falling in _____ autumn.

13 _____ children are making _____ snowman.

14 _____ water has got into _____ boat!

15 _____ horses are _____ useful animals.

16 The cook is frying _____ pork with _____ salted pepper.

17 Mr Lin is _____ teacher with many years of _____ experience.

18 He is _____ European. He is holding _____ English book.

19 She plays _____ squash and she also plays _____ tennis.

20 _____ science is making rapid progress in _____ China.

21 I live in _____ apartment. _____ apartment is new.

22 Johnson can run _____ mile in _____ five minutes.

23 The rocket is carrying _____ satellite into _____ space.

24 Judy's often absent from _____ school because of _____ illness.

25 What are _____ signs and symptoms of _____ mumps in children?

26 One small step for _____ man; one giant step for _____ mankind.

27 _____ pens I gave you were bought in _____ Italy.

28 _____ recognition is _____ greatest motivator.

29 It is impossible to see _____ elk* in _____ eucalyptus* tree.

30 I was in _____ Japanese restaurant. _____ restaurant served good food.

31 _____ church is on _____ left of _____ road.

32 There is _____ emergency exit at _____ end of _____ corridor.

33 We went to see _____ exhibition of _____ Chinese calligraphy at _____ museum.

34 Some animals, for example _____ cows and _____ sheep, eat _____ grass.

35 _____ Changjiang River is _____ third longest river in _____ world.

36 _____ cat owners often claim that _____ cats are more intelligent than _____ dogs.

37 _____ impressionism* is _____ 19th-century art movement that originated with _____ group of Paris-based artists.

*elk：麋，駝鹿    *eucalyptus：桉樹    *impressionism：印象主義，印象派

38 Kenya's Kiprop, _____ world's fastest man over 1,500 m this year, will have _____ one thing on his mind in London – to win _____ event properly.

39 _____ Gratitude* is _____ sign of _____ noble souls.

40 _____ river is 1,000 km long from _____ south to _____ north.

41 _____ summer usually begins in _____ June in this part of _____ world.

42 If I have had any _____ success, it's due to _____ luck, but I notice _____ harder I work, _____ luckier I get.

43 _____ Physics is _____ science of _____ matter and _____ energy.

44 _____ Phuket is _____ popular place for _____ snorkeling and _____ diving.

45 _____ hat and _____ coat cost $110 and _____ coat costs $100 more than _____ hat. How much does _____ coat cost?

46 He bought _____ new apartment in Mid-Levels. From _____ apartment, there is _____ marvellous view of _____ Victoria Harbour.

47 _____ success is not measured by _____ heights one attains, but by _____ obstacles one overcomes in its _____ attainment.

48 _____ man who is often called _____ America's greatest president was born on _____ February 12, 1809, in _____ crude log cabin in _____ Kentucky.

*gratitude：感激之情

49 _____ Lincolns were poor. They moved from one small farm to _____ another, trying to scratch out _____ living. When Abraham was seven, _____ family moved from Kentucky to _____ Indiana.

50 _____ lawyers work in a variety of _____ fields, from _____ criminal law to _____ divorce law to _____ patent law, navigating _____ legal system on _____ behalf of their clients.

# Section 3: Integrated Contextual Exercises

 綜合篇章練習

I　閱讀以下對話，並在適當處加上定冠詞（提示：必須加上 14 個定冠詞）。

## **Dialogue:**　Going to the airport

Cathy:　What's best way of getting to airport?

Eric:　Well, you can take airport bus.

Cathy:　Where do I catch it?

Eric:　There are special stops along this road. It's clearly signed.

Cathy:　How much is it from here?

Eric:　Oh, it's a fixed fare, and you need exact amount. Drivers don't give change. I think it' s about $30 from here.

Cathy:　But I've got piles of baggage.

Eric:　That's all right. They've got big luggage racks.

Cathy:　Is there any other way of getting there?

Eric:　Well, you could go by MTR, but it's awkward getting your luggage through barrier especially in rush hour, and nearest station is some 15 minutes away by bus from airport.

Cathy:　Oh, that's not a very good idea.

Eric:　Or you can take Airport Express. Trains are frequent and fast. It just takes you half an hour to get there from Central and it puts you down right by entrance of airport.

Cathy:　Great! They seem very convenient. I'd take Airport Express then. Well, I've got to check in at 2:15 so I thought I'd leave about now.

II 填空題 (在空格內填上 a、an、the 或 ∅)。

## The opening of A Tale Of Two Cities by Charles Dickens

IT WAS 1 _____ best of 2 _____ times, it was 3 _____ worst of 4 _____ times, it was 5 _____ age of 6 _____ wisdom, it was 7 _____ age of 8 _____ foolishness, it was 9 _____ epoch* of 10 _____ belief, it was 11 _____ epoch of 12 _____ incredulity*, it was 13 _____ season of 14 _____ Light, it was 15 _____ season of 16 _____ Darkness, it was 17 _____ spring of 18 _____ hope, it was 19 _____ winter of 20 _____ despair*, we had everything before us, we had nothing before us, we were all going direct to 21 _____ Heaven, we were all going direct 22 _____ other way – in 23 _____ short, 24 _____ period was so far like 25 _____ present period, that some of its 26 _____ noisiest authorities insisted on its being received, for 27 _____ good or for 28 _____ evil, in 29 _____ superlative degree of 30 _____ comparison only.

*epoch：時代，紀元　　*incredulity：懷疑，不相信　　*despair：絕望

III 填空題（在空格內填上 a、an、the 或 ∅）。

## Saving Sea Turtles

When 1 [ ] fishers put out their trawl nets* in 2 [ ] Gulf of Mexico and 3 [ ] South Atlantic, 4 [ ] sea turtles often end up trapped in 5 [ ] nets unintentionally. If 6 [ ] turtles cannot escape, they will drown. This is 7 [ ] major threat to 8 [ ] marine turtles and it is known as 9 [ ] bycatch*.

In 10 [ ] 1980s and 11 [ ] 1990s, 12 [ ] NOAA and 13 [ ] shrimp industry developed 14 [ ] turtle excluder devices. These devices direct 15 [ ] turtles toward 16 [ ] opening in 17 [ ] shrimp net, so they can escape. Each year 18 [ ] NOAA tests 19 [ ] new and improved turtle excluder device designs in 20 [ ] Panama City, 21 [ ] Florida, using 22 [ ] loggerhead turtles* raised in its Galveston, Texas, lab.

23 [ ] required use of turtle excluder devices has resulted in 24 [ ] almost 100 percent reduction in 25 [ ] turtle deaths due to 26 [ ] shrimp nets. 27 [ ] NOAA continues to work with 28 [ ] fishing industries all around 29 [ ] world to develop new techniques for preventing turtle bycatch and promoting 30 [ ] sustainable fishing operations.

*trawl nets：拖網　　*bycatch：混獲（漁夫在作業中意外撈到原本不打算捕獲的魚種）
*loggerhead turtles：紅海龜

IV 填空題（在空格內填入 a、an、the 或 ∅）。

## Death rate for cancer patients higher among men

NEW YORK (Reuters Health) — Not only are 1 _____ men more likely than 2 _____ women to be diagnosed with 3 _____ cancer, among those who get 4 _____ disease, men also have 5 _____ higher chance of dying from it, according to 6 _____ new study.

In 7 _____ analysis of cases of all but the sex-specific cancers like 8 _____ prostate* and ovarian* cancers, for example, men with the disease were more likely than women to die in each of 9 _____ past 10 years, researchers found.

That translates to 10 _____ extra 24,130 men dying of cancer in 2012 because of their gender.

"This gap needs to be closed," said Dr. Shahrokh Shariat from 11 _____ Weill Cornell Medical College in 12 _____ New York, who worked on the study.

"It's not about showing that men are only doing worse and, 'poor men.' It's about closing gender differences and improving 13 _____ health care" for both men and women, he said.

Using U.S. cancer registry data from 2003 through 2012, Shariat and his colleagues found 14 _____ ratio of deaths to cancer diagnoses decreased by 10 percent over 15 _____ past decade — but was consistently higher among

*prostate：前列線　　*ovarian：卵巢

men than women.

Overall, men with any type of cancer were six percent more likely to die of their disease than women with cancer. When men and women with 16 [____] same type of cancer were compared, that difference rose to more than 12 percent.

In 2012, 17 [____] Shariat's team calculated that about 575,130 men and 457,240 women would be diagnosed with 18 [____] non-sex specific cancer. Also this year, 19 [____] estimated 243,620 men will die of cancer – one death for every 2.36 new diagnoses – and 182,670 women will die, one for each 2.50 new diagnoses.

"We found that from 20 [____] 10 most common cancers in 21 [____] male and females...men present at a higher stage than females, and adjusted for the incidence, are more likely to die from the cancer," Shariat told Reuters Health.

"If you take 22 [____] average of 23 [____] 10 most common cancers, men are more likely to die in seven out of the ten," he added. In 24 [____] contrast, women are more likely to die only from bladder cancer, the researchers found.

25 [____] new study can't show what's behind the differences in cancer deaths, they wrote in The Journal of Urology.

But 26 ____ possible theories, they added, include men's higher rates of 27 ____ smoking and drinking combined with less frequent doctor's visits — which cause men's cancers to be diagnosed in later, more advanced stages.

28 ____ sex hormones may also contribute to differences in men's and women's immune systems, metabolism and general susceptibility to cancer, according to Yang Yang, 29 ____ sociologist and cancer researcher from 30 ____ University of North Carolina at 31 ____ Chapel Hill, who studies 32 ____ health disparities but wasn' t involved in 33 ____ new research.

She said 34 ____ new findings are consistent with work suggesting 35 ____ higher risk of death for men from many causes, including cancer.

"But 36 ____ full understanding of the origins and mechanisms in sex differences in cancer, as well as overall mortality has remained elusive," Yang told Reuters Health in 37 ____ email.

Shariat said men should be particularly proactive about their health care.

"That means going to screening programs, seeing a general practitioner or 38 ____ primary care provider on 39 ____ regular basis and as soon as 40 ____ symptoms arise that are new, mentioning that to their primary care physicians," he said.

SOURCE: The Journal of Urology, online December 3, 2012.

# Section 4: Creative Writing Exercises

 創意寫作：看漫畫，寫故事，想冠詞

## Exercise 01

# Time for change

請按每格的提示文字，以 50 字為限，運用正確冠詞寫出故事。

Jenny, clerk, same company, four years

new job, advertisement, newspaper

secretary, good money

call, appointment, interview

## xercise 02

# The amazing woodpecker

請按每格的提示文字，以 50 字為限，運用正確冠詞寫出故事。

woodpecker, interesting, amazing, bird

strong, pointed, beak, hammer

remove, bark, find, insects, eat

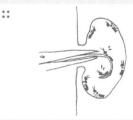

long tongue, four inches, sticky, tip, catch, insects

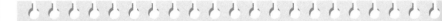

## Exercise 03

# Bob's Life

**請按每格的提示文字，以 50 字為限，運用正確冠詞寫出故事。**

Saturday nights, Bob, jog (noun), park

home, shower

dinner, newspaper, teach, son, violin

bed, midnight

## xercise 04

# A nightmare

請按每格的提示文字，以 50 字為限，運用正確冠詞寫出故事。

I, see, UFO, yesterday

aliens, come out, dressed, black, taller than

shorter one, catch me, arm, shout

policeman, come to rescue, be killed, taller

_____

_____

_____

_____

_____

_____

_____

# Section 5: Advanced Level

 進階：冠詞與限定詞的關係

## ❂ 甚麼是 determiner（限定詞）？

冠詞是限定詞的一種。限定詞用來限定名詞所指的範圍，如使名詞變成泛指、特指或說明數量。除了冠詞以外，英語的其他限定詞還包括 demonstrative（指示代詞）、 possessive noun（名詞所有格）、possessive adjective（所有格形容詞）、number（數詞）、 quantifier（數量詞）與某些形容詞性的物主代詞。

這些限定詞扮演着相同的語法功能。一般來說，在單數可數名詞之前都需要有一個限定詞。從功能上來說，限定詞可分為兩類。第一類是有助於分類或確認的限定詞，第二類是能夠表示數量的限定詞。

### 有助於分類或確認的限定詞包括以下五種：

1 不定冠詞 a、an

例
- Liz bought a new smartphone yesterday.
  昨天麗絲買了一部新的智能手機。（但不必說明是哪一部。）

2 定冠詞 the

例
- The smartphone Liz is using is a new one.
  麗絲用的這部智能手機是全新的。
  （特指是哪一部智能手機。）

3 指示代詞 this、 that、 these、 those 等

例
- Liz bought this / that smartphone yesterday.
  昨天麗絲買了這部 / 那部智能手機。
  （即是我指給你看的那部。）

4 名詞所有格 Bob's、 Christine's、 his friend's、
  five minutes' 等

例
- What do you think about Liz's new smartphone?
  你覺得麗絲的新智能手機怎樣？
  （即是明確指出屬於某某的那部。）

5 所有格形容詞 my、your、his、her、their 等

• What do you think about her new smartphone?
你覺得她的新智能手機怎樣？
（即是從上下文判斷是屬於某某的那部。）

**能夠表示數量的限定詞包括兩種：**

1 數詞 one、two、three 等

• Liz bought two new smartphones yesterday.
昨天麗絲買了兩部新智能手機。
（即是說明購買的具體數量。）

2 數量詞 some、any、many、much、few、little、
plenty of、a lot of、none of the 等

• Liz bought some new smartphones yesterday.
昨天麗絲買了幾部新智能手機。
• Liz didn't buy many new smartphones yesterday.
昨天麗絲沒有買多少新的智能手機。
（即是說明購買的大致數量。）

## ✚ 不定冠詞 a / an 和數詞 one 的區別

不定冠詞 a / an 與數詞 one 同源，表示 "一" 的意義，但 a / an 不強調數目觀念。在英文中，a / an 並不等於 one。

- Liz bought a new smartphone yesterday.
  （不具體指明哪一部。）

- Liz bought one new smartphone yesterday, not two.
  （指明是一部，與 two、three 等相對而言。）

※ 注意，one 不能指「任何一個」(不具體指明哪一個)，如下面一句不能用 one：

× I am one Chinese.

✓ I am a Chinese. 我是（一個）中國人。

× This is one apple.

✓ This is an apple. 這是（一個）蘋果。

one 強調數目觀念，如下面一句用 one 比用 a / an 更好：

✓ One minute is enough for me. 給我一分鐘就足夠了。

? A minute is enough for me.

只有在表示數字的情況時，a / an 與 one 方可互相替換使用：

## 整數：

| 基數 | 寫法 / 讀法 |
| --- | --- |
| 100 | a [one] hundred 一百 |
| 1, 000 | a [one] thousand 一千 |
| 100, 000 | a [one] hundred thousand 十萬 |
| 1, 000, 000 | a [one] million 一百萬 |
| 100, 000, 000 | a [one] hundred million 一億 |
| 1, 000, 000, 000 | a [one] thousand million OR a [one] billion 十億 |

## 分數：

| 分數 | 寫法 / 讀法 |
| --- | --- |
| 1/2 | a [one] half 二分之一；一半 |
| 1/3 | a [one] third 三分之一 |
| 1/4 | a [one] quarter; a [one] fourth 四分之一 |
| 1/5 | a [one] fifth 五分之一 |
| 1/6 | a [one] sixth 六分之一 |
| 1/7 | a [one] seventh 七分之一 |
| 1/8 | an [one] eighth 八分之一 |
| 1/9 | a [one] ninth 九分之一 |
| 1/10 | a [one] tenth 十分之一 |

注意，以上用法可引伸至金錢或度量衡的表示方式，例如a [one] thousand miles（一千公里）、a [one] hundred thousand dollars（十萬元）等。

## ⊕ 限定詞的位置

名詞或名詞短語前面，通常只用一個限定詞，換個角度來說，一個名詞短語裏的第一個詞都是限定詞。

- a new smartphone 一部新的智慧手機
- the enthusiastic audience 熱情的觀眾
- those homemade cakes 那些自家製糕點
- their friendly neighbours 他們友善的鄰居
- his friend's birthday party 他朋友的生日派對
- five minutes' walk 五分鐘的步行
- ten Chinese books 十本中文書
- many funny people 很多有趣的人

※ 注意，一個名詞或名詞短語前，永遠不會放兩個限定詞。例如我們可以說 my phone 或 the phone 或 this phone，但不可能同時放兩個像 a、the、my、your、Jason's、this、that、those 等的限定詞：

✗ **my the** new smartphone

✗ **his this** smartphone

✗ **Liz's her** smartphone

### ⊕ 前限定詞 + 定冠詞

英語還有一些詞語叫 pre-determiner（前限定詞），它們則可以放在定冠詞或其他限定詞之前。

前限定詞的例子包括 all、both 和 half。

- **All** new smartphones are expensive.
- **All the** new smartphones are expensive.
- **All of the** new smartphones are expensive.
  （第一句裏的 all 是泛指；而第二三句則可以互相替代，指特定數量的智能手機）

- **Both** smartphones are expensive.
- **Both the** smartphones are expensive.
- **Both of the** smartphones are expensive.
  （第一句裏的 both 意指「不只一個，還有另一個」；第二三句可以互相替代，both 與 the 連用時，指的是某些特定事物，譬如 the new smartphones produced by Samsung。）

- **Half the** new smartphones are sold to China.
- **Half of the** new smartphones are sold to China
  （兩句可以互相替代，表示特定數量的智能手機）

# 練習答案
Answers

SECTION 2: INTEGRATED SENTENCE EXERCISES 綜合句子練習

I

1 an  2 a  3 Ø  4 an  5 Ø  6 Ø  7 Ø  8 a  9 Ø  10 Ø  11 a  12 Ø  13 Ø  14 the
15 A / The  16 Ø  17 a  18 Ø  19 an  20 Ø  21 the  22 the  23 Ø  24 Ø  25 Ø
26 the  27 the  28 Ø  29 A  30 the  31 the  32 Ø  33 the  34 the  35 the  36 Ø
37 Ø  38 Ø  39 Ø  40 the  41 the Ø  42 a  43 Ø  44 Ø  45 Ø  46 Ø  47 the
48 Ø  49 a  50 a

II

1 Trees don't grow in the (Antarctic).  2 These keys are (the only ones) I've
got.  3 I bought (a beautiful cup and saucer).  4 He (went to prison) for arson.
5 (A policeman) is waiting for you at the door. 6. (I've got a) sore throat.
7 My brother (is an architect).  8 (The architect who designed this bridge)
won a prize.  9 (A Mr Zhu / Chu) left a message for you.  10 (Museums) in
Hong Kong are closed (on Tuesdays).

III

1 delete "A"  2 add "the" before violin  3 delete "the"  4 delete "the"
5 change "a" to "an"  6 add "The" before pandas  7 delete "a"  8 add "a"
before piece 9  delete "The"  10 add "the" before Philippines  11 change "A"
to "The"; add "a" before walk  12 change "a" to "the"  13 Delete "The"
before honesty; add "the" before "best  14 delete "the" before bus

15 delete "the" before dawn  16 add "The" before Spring Festival; add "the" before time; delete "the" before family  17 add "An" before SOS; change "a" to "an" before international  18 change "a" to "the"  19 change "a" to "the"  20 delete "the"

IV

1 A, a  2 a, Ø  3 a, an  4 a, Ø  5 A, a  6 an, a  7 a, Ø  8 a, Ø

9 Ø / the, the  10 a, Ø  11 a, the  12 Ø, Ø  13 The, a  14 Ø, the  15 Ø, Ø

16 Ø, Ø  17 a, Ø  18 a, an  19 Ø, Ø  20 Ø, Ø  21 an, The  22 a, Ø

23 a, Ø  24 Ø, Ø  25 the, Ø  26 Ø, Ø  27 The, Ø  28 Ø, the  29 an, a  30 a, The

31 The, the, the  32 an, the, the  33 an, Ø, the

34 Ø, Ø, Ø  35 The / Ø, the, the  36 Ø , Ø , Ø  37 Ø, a, a

38 the, Ø, the  39 Ø, the, Ø  40 The, Ø, Ø  41 Ø, Ø, the

42 Ø, Ø, the, the  43 Ø, the, Ø, Ø  44 Ø, a, Ø, Ø

45 A, Ø, the, the, the  46 a, the, a, Ø / the  47 Ø, the, the, Ø

48 The, Ø, Ø,a, Ø  49 The, Ø,a, the,  Ø  50 Ø, Ø, Ø, Ø, Ø, the, Ø

## SECTION 3: INTEGRATED CONTEXTUAL EXERCISES 綜合篇章練習

I

Cathy: What's (the) best way of getting to (the) airport?

Eric: Well, you can take (the) airport bus.

Cathy: Where do I catch it?

Eric: There are special stops along this road. It's clearly signed.

Cathy: How much is it from here?

Eric: Oh, it's a fixed fare, and you need (the) exact amount. (The) drivers don't give change. I think it's about $30 from here.

Cathy: But I've got piles of baggage.

Eric: That's all right. They've got big luggage racks.

Cathy: Is there any other way of getting there?

Eric: Well, you could go by MTR, but it's awkward getting your luggage through (the) barrier especially in (the) rush hour, and (the) nearest station is some 15 minutes away by bus from (the) airport.

Cathy: Oh, that's not a very good idea.

Eric: Or you can take (the) Airport Express. (The) trains are frequent and fast. It just takes you half an hour to get there from Central and it puts you down right by (the) entrance of (the) airport.

Cathy: Great! They seem very convenient. I'd take (the) Airport Express then. Well, I've got to check in at 2:15 so I thought I'd leave about now.

II

1 the  2 Ø  3 the  4 Ø  5 the  6 Ø  7 the  8 Ø  9 the  10 Ø  11 the  12 Ø

13 the  14 Ø  15 the  16 Ø  17 the  18 Ø  19 the  20 Ø  21 Ø  22 the  23 Ø

24 the  25 the  26 Ø  27 Ø  28 Ø  29 the  30 Ø

III

1 Ø  2 the  3 Ø  4 Ø  5 the  6 the  7 a  8 Ø  9 Ø  10 the  11 Ø

12 Ø  13 the  14 Ø  15 Ø  16 an  17 the  18 Ø  19 the  20 Ø  21 Ø  22 Ø  23

The  24 an  25 Ø  26 Ø  27 Ø  28 Ø  29 the  30 Ø

IV

1 Ø  2 Ø  3 Ø  4 the  5 a  6 a  7 an  8 Ø  9 the  10 an  11 Ø

12 Ø  13 Ø  14 the  15 the  16 the  17 Ø  18 a  19 an  20 the

21 Ø  22 an  23 the  24 Ø  25 The  26 Ø  27 Ø  28 Ø  29 a

30 the  31 Ø  32 Ø  33 the  34 the  35 a  36 a  37 an  38 Ø  39 a  40 Ø

Section 4: Creative Writing Exercises 創意寫作：看漫畫，寫故事，想冠詞

(Suggested Answers)

**Ex 1:** Jenny is **a** clerk. She has worked at **the** same company for **Ø** four years. Now she wants **a** new job. She saw **an** ad in **the** newspaper for **a** job that pays **Ø** good money. They are looking for **a** secretary. Jenny called **the** company and made **an** appointment for **an** interview.

**Ex 2: The** woodpecker is **an** interesting and amazing bird. It has **a** strong, pointed beak. It acts as **a** hammer to remove **Ø** bark from **Ø** trees and find **Ø** insects to eat. It also has **a** very long tongue which is up to **Ø** four inches long. It is sticky on **the** tip for catching **Ø** insects.

**Ex 3:** On **Ø** Saturday nights, Bob usually goes for **a** jog at **a** park nearby. At **a** quarter to eight, he goes **Ø** home and takes **a** shower. Then, he has his dinner and reads **the** newspaper. After **Ø** dinner, he teaches his son to play **the** violin. He goes to **Ø** bed at **Ø** midnight.

**Ex 4:** I saw **a** UFO yesterday. Two aliens came out of it. They were dressed in **Ø** black. One is taller than **the** other. **The** shorter one caught me by **the** arm. I shouted for **Ø** help. **A** policeman came to my rescue, but was killed by **the** taller of **the** two aliens.